LOOPS AND LONG LONG LINES

Lucy Scarlett Strutt

For Marie, my reason

With special thanks to Simon Murray
for his guidance and support

First published in 2021

Text and illustrations copyright © Lucy Scarlett Strutt 2021

The right of Lucy Scarlett Strutt to be identified as the
author and illustrator of this work has been asserted
by her in accordance with the Copyright,
Designs and Patents Act 1988.

A CIP catalogue record for this book is available from the British Library

ISBN 978-1-9168702-0-8

www.theartinscarlett.com

Printed in China by Leo Paper Products Ltd

Dedicated to my family and friends,

to those that try and keep on trying,

to the brave and to the kind.

This tank is far too small
said the turtle to the turtle.
I think said the turtle
that we are just too big...

much too **big** to fit in

this tank in which we turtles

try to swim.

But they tried and kept on trying

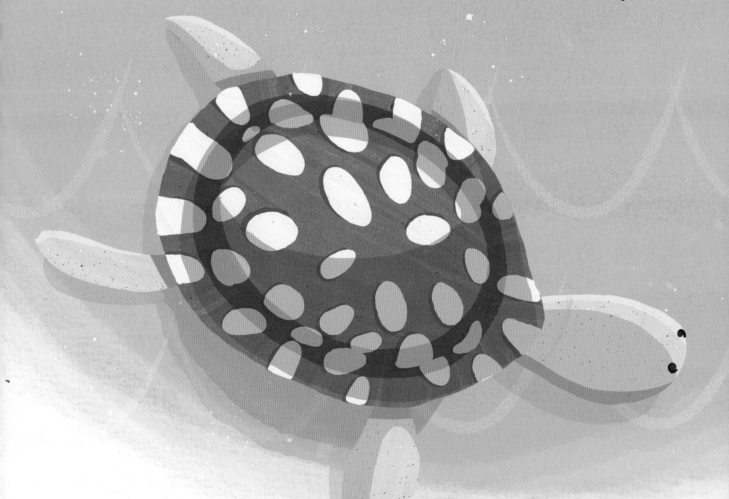

swimming on and on in circles

with their shells above the water line

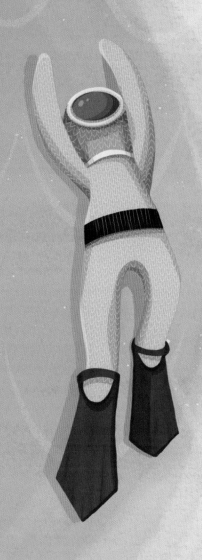

and feet touching the floor.

The turtle told the turtle
that once upon a time,
the tank was **big** and so they swam
in loops and . . .

a l o n g , l o n g . l i n e ·

The trouble is we grew

said the turtle and I know

that this space gets so much smaller

the **bigger** we both grow.

I see the turtle said

but somehow the turtle had

forgotten how it used to be

and felt so very sad.

Don't be so sad the turtle said

for I have seen somewhere . . .

a somewhere so much **bigger**
by about a B I L L I O N times,
where we can swim around all day
in loops and . . .

long, long lines.

That somewhere sounds so **big**
said the turtle,
is it near
or a l o n g, lo n g way
away from here?

I'm not sure said the turtle
with a puzzled sort of look . . .

I just saw what I saw

on a page in a book.

Oh I see it said the turtle
how the water goes and goes,
I wonder if somebody knows
that we turtles swim in circles
with our shells above the water line
and feet touching the floor.

I hope so said the turtle
with a far off look of dread.
I fear if we stay here too long
we might both end up . . .

don't say that

said the turtle to the turtle,

don't be gloomy.

We must try to get out

and find somewhere more roomy!

I agree came a voice

they had not heard before,

from somewhere below

their feet touching the floor.

The turtle looked down
and said who are you?
I'm a snail said the snail
and I'm stuck in here too.

How sorry we are said the turtle

but we did not see you there,

that's quite alright the snail replied

I am rather small to be fair.

Well now that we know
you are stuck in here too,
have you any idea
what on earth we should do?

I think we need a plan
said the snail,
so they began
to think in fact they thought
a **thousand** things.

Though most were quite impossible
as turtles don't have wings.

They were running out of time now,
running out of thinking,
either they were getting **bigger** still
or the tank was shrinking.

I'm afraid said the turtle
that we might just have to stay
because that somewhere so much **bigger**

seems so very far away.

A BILLION

times too far away
and that's too many times.
I don't think we'll ever swim
in loops and . . .

long, long lines.

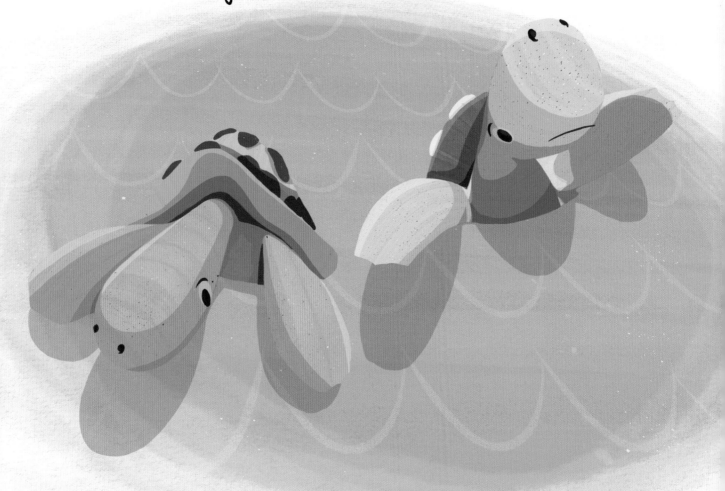

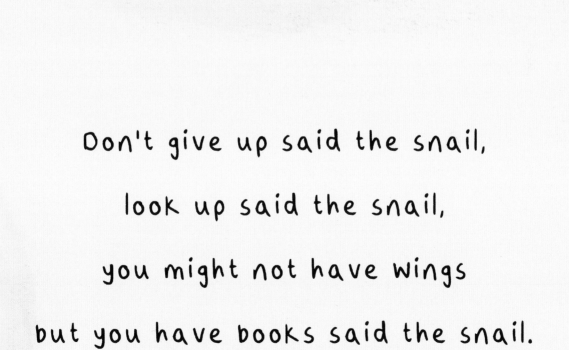

Don't give up said the snail,

look up said the snail,

you might not have wings

but you have books said the snail.

"THIS TANK MIGHT WELL BE FAR TOO SMALL

BUT THAT JUST LOOKS . . . .

TOO HIGH!"

SAID THE TURTLE TO THE SNAIL WITH A SIGH

We could try
said the turtle to the turtle.

So they tried...

This place is far too **big** . . .